JUDY MOODY AND FRIENDS
Triple Pet Trouble

Megan McDonald
illustrated by Erwin Madrid

based on the characters
created by Peter H. Reynolds

CANDLEWICK PRESS

For the helpful crew at California Carnivores
M. M.

To my wife, Hoài
E. M.

Text copyright © 2015 by Megan McDonald
Illustrations copyright © 2015 by Peter H. Reynolds
Judy Moody font copyright © 2003 by Peter H. Reynolds

Judy Moody®. Judy Moody is a registered trademark of Candlewick Press, Inc.

First edition 2015

Library of Congress Catalog Card Number 2014955349
ISBN 978-0-7636-7443-4 (hardcover)
ISBN 978-0-7636-7615-5 (paperback)

16 17 18 19 20 APS 10 9 8 7 6 5 4 3

Printed in Humen, Dongguan, China

This book was typeset in ITC Stone Informal.
The illustrations were created digitally.

Candlewick Press
99 Dover Street
Somerville, Massachusetts 02144

visit us at www.candlewick.com

CONTENTS

CHAPTER 1
Jaws in Love

Jaws looked droopy. Jaws looked mopey. Jaws looked wilty. Jaws was Judy Moody's Venus flytrap. Two of his leaves were turning black. One of his traps was turning dead.

Judy Moody stuck her Grouchy pencil in one of his traps and . . . *snap . . . trap . . . NOT!* Jaws did not snap his trap. Not even when she tried an ant, a tiny cricket, or a roly-poly.

Stink's jaw dropped when he saw Judy's pet. "What's wrong with Jaws? He looks like moldy old bread."

"He's sick," said Judy.

"Ooh. Maybe he has the measles."

"I don't get it," said Judy. "I feed him earwigs from Dad's garden. I take him outside in winter. I snip off his dead leaves when they turn black."

"Maybe he doesn't like his new haircut," said Stink.

"I know," said Judy. "Dr. Judy, Pet Vet, to the rescue!"

Dr. Judy gave Jaws a bath—with rainwater.

She sang him the Baby Bumble Bee song.

She read to him from *Charlotte's Web*.

4

"Don't read him a sad book!" said Stink.

"It's his favorite," said Judy. But Jaws looked as droopy as ever.

Judy looked stuff up in her *Big Head Book of Bug-Eating Plants*. "It says here that there's only one place in the world where Venus flytraps grow in nature."

"Where?"

"A place called Cape Fear," said Judy, "in North Carolina."

Stink shivered. The Moodys' cat, Mouse, pulled her toy mouse in closer.

"Maybe Jaws is homesick," said Stink.

"Maybe Jaws is just lonely," Judy said.

"Aha! Jaws needs a friend," said Stink. He ran downstairs and came back carrying a fishbowl. A goldfish was floating on top of the sloshing water.

Stink set the bowl down next to Jaws. "Jaws, meet your new friend, Goldilocks."

Judy peered into the bowl. "Stink. That's no goldfish. That's a cracker. A goldfish-shaped cracker."

"Jaws doesn't know that," whispered Stink.

"He'd probably rather *eat* than *meet* his new friend," Judy whispered back.

Jaws did not perk up one bit.

"It's not working," said Stink.

"Making friends takes time," said Judy.

Judy and Stink gave it time.
One day. Two days. Three days.
Judy peered into the goldfish bowl.
"Goldilocks looks puffy," said Judy,
"and pale."

"Let me see," said Stink, pulling the
fishbowl toward him. The cracker fell
to pieces. "Argh! Jaws's new friend
just became five friends!" cried Stink.

"Jaws looks worse," said Judy.

"You'd look bad, too, if your best friend just turned into Cream of Goldfish," said Stink.

"Let's move Jaws over to the window," said Judy. "I think he needs more light."

They set Jaws down on the window seat next to Mouse and a pile of papers and junk. "Move over, Mouse," said Judy. "Make way for Jaws."

Mouse leaped to the floor, but a piece of paper got stuck to her paw. Junk mail! Mouse shook her paw, trying to get rid of it.

"Mouse is trying to show us something," said Stink.

Judy unstuck the piece of junk mail from Mouse's paw. On the flyer were pictures of a Venus flytrap, a pitcher plant, a sundew, and a cobra lily. *Carnivore city!*

The flyer said GRAND OPENING! The flyer said that a store called Cape Fear Carnivores was opening right there in Frog Neck Lake!

Judy kissed her cat on the nose. She, Dr. Judy Moody, knew just what to do to save Jaws.

Judy and her dad took Jaws to Cape Fear Carnivores. Judy talked to the owner, Peter Tomato. Peter Tomato knew everything in the world about bug-eating plants.

Peter Tomato helped Judy start her very own bog. First she picked out a pot that looked like a mini bathtub. Next she filled it with sand and peat moss. Then she planted Jaws in the bog next to a brand-new, way-tall, red-and-green North American pitcher plant.

"Jaws," said Judy, "meet Petunia, your new bug-eating buddy!"

When Judy and Jaws and Petunia got home, Stink peered into one of the pitcher plant's long tubes.

"There's water in there," said Stink, "and a dead fly."

"That's how a pitcher plant traps its food," said Judy. "An insect smells nectar, lands on the mouth of the plant, and—*zoom*—falls right down into the tube."

"Cool," said Stink.

"Did you know some pitcher plants eat animal poop? They like shrew poo."

"Hardee-har-har," said Stink. "You made that up."

"Did not!" said Judy. "Peter Tomato at Cape Fear Carnivores told me. Peter Tomato would not lie."

Judy sat back to admire her bog. Jaws did not look droopy or mopey or wilty. Jaws looked positively perky.

At last, Jaws had company. He curled a leaf around Petunia, the pitcher plant.

"Look," said Judy. "I think Jaws is in love!"

"Love at first sight," said Stink.

"Love at first bite," said Judy.

CHAPTER 2
Mystic Mouse

Judy was reading to Mouse from her
Big Head Book of Pets. She was reading
all about parrots and potbellied pigs
and pocket pets—pets that can fit in
a pocket.

Then she looked out the window.
"Check it out, Mouse. Stink has a
lemonade stand. And his lemonade
stand has a big long line."

Jingle-jangle. "I can already hear the jingle of all the quarters in Stink's pockets."

All of a sudden, she, Judy Moody, had an idea. A pockets-full-of-quarters idea.

She set up a table down the sidewalk from Stink. She hung up a sign. She put out an empty jar. She hid her *Big Head Book of Pets* under the table, just in case.

"Hey!" said Stink. "This is my corner."

"It's a free country, Stink."

"Why is Mouse wearing a turban and sitting on your mood pillow like a queen?"

PET PSYCHIC:
Mouse the
Mind Reader

Judy pointed to her sign. PET
PSYCHIC: MOUSE THE MIND READER.
"Mouse knows what other pets are
thinking. She knew Jaws needed a
friend, remember?"

"What's the jar for?"

"The jar is for when all the quarters
start to roll in. Twenty-five cents a
reading."

Stink went back to his table. "Ice-cold lemonade!" cried Stink. "Hand-stirred. Only twenty-five cents!"

"Meet pet psychic Mouse Moody!" called Judy. "Got a pet problem? Mouse can solve it!"

Kids gawked at Mouse on their way to get lemonade but didn't stop. Judy put up more signs. FREE TUMMY RUBS! FREE HEAD SCRATCHES!

FREE TUMMY RUBS!

PET PSYCHIC: Mouse the Mind Reader

Rocky was first in line. "Hi, Rock," said Judy. "What's your pet problem?"

Rocky held out his pet iguana. "It's Houdini. He turned a weird color. And his skin is peeling."

Judy ducked under the table to peek at her Big Head book in secret. She sprang back up and leaned over her cat. "Mouse the Mind Reader

FREE
HEAD
SCRATCHES!

has spoken. She says Houdini is just
growing. That's why he's shedding his
skin." Judy scratched the back of the
iguana's head. "Give him a nice bath,
mist him every morning, and he'll
feel better."

"Thanks!" said Rocky.

"Twenty-five cents, please," said
Judy. *Ka-ching!*

Behind Rocky was Frank Pearl. His parrot, Cookie, sat on his shoulder.

Judy gave Cookie a free tummy rub while Frank told Judy the problem. "My parrot hates my sister," said Frank. "Every time my sister gets too close, Cookie bites her."

"Let me ask Mouse the Mind Reader," said Judy.

"I think your mind reader is sleeping," said Frank.

FREE TUMMY RUBS!

PET PSYCHIC: Mouse the Mind Reader

"She's not sleeping. She's thinking," said Judy, putting her ear up to Mouse.

"Mouse the Magnificent says it's all about the treats. Do a fun trick with Cookie, but let *your sister* give her a treat."

"Mouse told you all that?" said Frank. "Wow!" He dropped a quarter in the jar.

FREE
HEAD
CRATCHES!

Next in line were Amy Namey and Jessica Finch. "I don't have a pet," said Amy.

Mouse curled her tail into a question mark. Judy said, "Mouse the Magnificent says, How about a pocket pet? Sugar gliders are cute. They fit in your pocket. Or a goldfish. *Not* the cracker kind. Twenty-five cents, please."

"But I'm not here about a pet for me," said Amy. "I'm here about PeeGee." She pointed to Jessica Finch's potbellied pig on a leash.

"PeeGee is freaking out," Jessica told Judy. "Every time he comes into my room, he knocks over my chair and chews my shoes and squeals like a—"

"Pig?" asked Judy.

Jessica nodded.

"Got that, Mouse?" Judy said. Mouse purred. Mouse purred some more.

"Mouse is thinking," said Judy.

"How do you know what she's thinking?" asked Jessica.

"Mouse and I are of one mind. It sounds to me—I mean to Mouse—like *somebody* needs to learn a few rules at obedience school."

"I love rules!" said Jessica. "And obedience. Maybe I can teach PeeGee myself."

Clink. Clink. Clink-clink-clink. The quarters kept on coming.

Mouse helped a parakeet with no tweet (Hello! Turn on the light),

a fish with ick, a.k.a. measles (Hello! Get fish medicine from the pet store),

and a pet rock that lost one googly
eye (Hello, glue!).

Mouse was a regular Dr. Dolittle,
an animal whisperer of the third
kind, a pet psychic with a sixth sense.

Judy jingled and jangled the
quarters in her jar for Stink to hear.

"Hey!" said Stink. "You're stealing
all my customers. Everybody wants
to see Mouse the Mystic. Nobody's
thirsty anymore."

32

Judy held up Mouse's water bowl for everyone to see. "Mouse the Mystic will now gaze into the Eternal Water Bowl of Serenity."

FREE TUMMY RUBS!

PET PSYCHIC: Mouse the ___l Reader

FREE HEAD SCRATCHES!

Mouse twitched her whiskers. Mouse licked her lips. "Mouse feels a great thirst coming on," said Judy.

Mouse stuck out her tongue and lapped up water like crazy.

A hush fell over the crowd. Everyone gazed at Mouse the Mind Reader.

"Come to think of it," said Frank, "I feel thirsty, too."

"Me, too," said Rocky and Amy at the same time.

"Me, three," said Jessica Finch. "PeeGee's thirsty, too."

Now everybody rushed to get in
line at Stink's table. In two minutes
flat, Stink ran out of lemonade. He
ran into the house and came back
carrying a pitcher of water.

LEMONADE

"Ice-cold water!" Stink yelled. "From the Eternal Fountain of Thirst Quenching. Hand-stirred! Only twenty-five cents a cup!"

CHAPTER 3
Toady and the Vampire

Zing! Toady zinged off Judy's bottom bunk bed. *Boing!* He boinged off her finger-knitting yarn. Stink's pet toad, Toady, was going nutso, zinging and boinging all over the place.

Judy scooped him up, then squished into her window seat between Mouse and the bog buddies, Jaws and Petunia.

EEW! All of a sudden, Judy felt something warm and wet in her hand. *Gross-o-rama!* She set the toad down.

Toady made
a puddle on her
mood pillow.
"Bad Toady!"
Judy said.

Then he made a puddle on top of her gumball machine. "Bad, bad Toady!" Judy said.

He made a puddle in the middle of her squiggle rug.

"That does it!" said Judy. "You and I are going on a field trip."

Judy rode Toady to Jessica Finch's house on her bike. A sign in the yard said JESSICA FINCH'S DOGGY DAY CARE AND OBEDIENCE SCHOOL.

JESSICA FINCH'S
DOGGY
DAY CARE
AND
OBEDIENCE
SCHOOL

Judy did not see a single dog. She did see Houdini, Rocky's iguana; Cookie, Frank's parrot; and PeeGee WeeGee, Jessica's pig, running around like crazy. Jessica was shouting, "Sit," "Stay," and "Heel," but none of them listened. None of them behaved.

This looked more like DIS-obedience school!

Jessica Finch and Amy Namey ran over to Judy. A stripe-faced fur ball with dark eyes and a pink nose stuck its head out of Amy's pocket. "Meet Boo," said Amy. "It's short for Peek-a-Boo."

"You got a sugar glider?" asked Judy. "You lucky dog!"

"How come *you're* here?" Jessica asked Judy.

"Toady's being a bad toad today." Judy told them about the toad pee on everything. "Will you take one more student?"

Jessica frowned. Jessica hemmed and hawed.

"Don't be a toadstool," said Judy.

"Okay. He can stay."

"Sit!" Jessica said to the animals. Houdini crawled away.

"Sit!" Jessica said again. Cookie hopped up and down and clacked her beak.

"Sit!" PeeGee just chased his tail.

"Sit!" Boo jumped out of Amy's pocket and knocked over his barrel of toy monkeys.

"Sit!" said Jessica. Toady sat.

Judy clapped her hands. "Toady!
You did it!"

"Stay!" said Jessica. Houdini crawled under a pile of leaves.

"Stay!" Jessica called again. Cookie flapped her wings and flew onto Judy's head.

"Stay!" PeeGee chased his tail some more.

"Stay!" Boo glided through the air and landed on PeeGee.

"Stay!" Jessica told Toady. Toady stayed.

"Good Toady!" Judy yelled.

Jessica held up a Hula-Hoop. "Jump!" she said. PeeGee chased after a ball. "Bad pig!" yelled Jessica. Boo chased after PeeGee. Cookie chased after Boo.

Jessica tried again. "Jump!" Toady jumped . . . right through the Hula-Hoop!

"You're good at getting Toady to obey," said Judy.

"Gold star for you, Toady." Jessica held him in her hand. "I still want to be in your Toad Pee Club," she said to the toad, "but you won't even pee on me."

"Toady gets an A-plus for Toad School," said Judy.

"That'll be one dollar," said Jessica Finch.

"Will you take four quarters?" Judy asked.

The next day, Judy teased Toady about obedience school. "You are *toadally* teacher's pet!" she said. All of a sudden, she felt something warm and wet on her hand. *Eew!* That naughty toad sprang out of her hand and hopped under the bed.

Judy heard a voice. "Hey, Judy! Want to go monster hunting?" It was Amy Namey.

"I *am* monster hunting," said Judy. She rescued Toady and dusted him off. "*This* monster. Toady acted perfect at obedience school. But the second I got him home, he turned into a little monster again. I don't get it."

Amy wasn't listening. Amy was staring. Amy was pointing at Judy's

new plant on the window seat. "You have a pitcher plant? I saw one in Borneo. It had one of those long scary names like *Carnivoria vampira* or something."

"This isn't a vampire," said Judy. "This is a new friend for Jaws. Her name is Petunia."

"Uh-oh," said Amy.

"What-oh?" asked Judy. She set Toady down on her top bunk.

"Um, I hate to tell you this, but . . . some giant pitcher plants can eat a frog."

Judy sprang up. *A frog-eating pitcher plant? Gulp!*

"Or a mouse or a rat," said Amy, "or a . . . *toad!*"

"No wonder Toady's been acting psycho," said Judy. "He's scared of Petunia, the vampire pitcher plant!"

Judy turned to look at Toady—
Wait! Toady? Where was that toad now?

Judy rushed over to Petunia. "Open wide and say 'Ahh'!" Judy said in her best doctor voice. She looked down Petunia's throat.

Judy did not see a bug. She did not see a spider, ant, or earwig. She saw a puddle. A small puddle of liquid. Amy saw it, too.

Was it . . . could it be . . . toad pee?

"ROAR!" said Judy. "The vampire plant ate Toady!"

Just then, Stink came running into Judy's room. "*Who* ate Toady?" he asked.

"Nobody."

"Where is he, then?"

"Um . . ." said Judy.

Just then, Toady hopped from the bedpost to the desk to the doorknob.

"Right there," said Amy, pointing.

Stink scooped him up. "Phew. Don't scare me like that."

Judy pushed Stink and Toady toward the door. "Stink! Get him out of here! My room is now officially a FROG-FREE zone."

"A toad is not a frog," said Stink.

"Tell that to the *Toadivoria vampira!*" said Judy.

"The *toadi*-huh?"

Judy pointed to the pitcher plant. "Stink, I hate to tell you this. But Jaws's new BFF is a freaky, frog-eating vampire. No lie. Say hello to Count Petunia."